U0023368

丁丁企鵝遊學館

閱亮點
ENRICH SPOT

丁丁企鵝遊學館

有o情有t境 學英語

05 世界篇 Hello World

原作 江記 · 撰文 閱亮點編輯室

Contents
目錄

Meet the characters
角色介紹

Ding Ding
A little penguin.
He is a lively kid
who is ready to play
at all times!

Mum
Ding Ding's mother.
She always teaches
Ding Ding to be
a well-behaved child.

Dad
Ding Ding's father.
He loves his family
so much.

Mushroom

A friend of Ding Ding.
Her hairstyle makes her
look like a mushroom!

Ryan

Ding Ding's cousin.
He is a mature penguin
for his age.

Masihung

A bear who wears a mask on his face.
He goes beyond lazy and
into super lazy!

Panda

A roommate of Masihung.
He is a conscientious panda. Sadly,
he is worlds apart from Masihung.

Come rain or shine 風雨不改

1 Go on the trip 去旅行

2 No matter the weather
任何天氣都沒關係

3 Right away 立即

⚪💬 Weather forecast 天氣預報

1. What will the weather be tomorrow?
明天的天氣怎樣？

2. Should have 好應該

3. (Not)... anymore （不）再

Wow! The sun is finally coming out!

I love spending time in the sunshine, especially when we're on vacation.

1 In the sunshine 在陽光下

2 On vacation 渡假

Claiming the baggage 領取行李

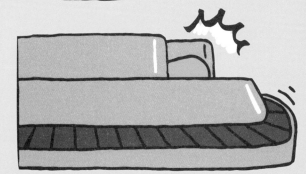

Sightseeing 觀光

Where should we go sightseeing today?

1 Walk along the seashore 沿岸散步   **2** Shall we…? 我們可以……嗎？

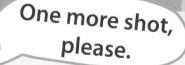

1 No problem. 沒問題。

2 Shot 照片

Taking pictures 拍照片 ②

1 Smile wide.
笑得燦爛點。

2 Adorable 很可愛

Travelling around the world
環遊世界

Australia 澳洲

1 Hop（動物）蹦跳　2 Pouch 育兒袋　3 High five! 擊掌吧！

1 What fun! 真開心！

2 Let's party! 盡情狂歡吧！

China 中國

1 The Great Wall 萬里長城

2 The Forbidden City 故宮

Canada 加拿大

1 Ski 滑雪

2 Roll down the slope 滾下斜坡

Easter Island 復活節島

1 Dozens of 很多

2 Statue 雕像

3 So what? 那又怎樣？

Finland 芬蘭

1 Aurora 極光

2 I don't think so.
我不認同。

3 Long to
很想、渴望

Someone's flying through the aurora! Are they Santa Claus and his reindeers?

I don't think so, because we're here!

HO, HO, HO!

Oh, there you are! I've been longing to meet you!

Japan 日本

Japanese Ramen Noodles Restaurant

Japan is famous for its unique cuisine, such as sushi and ramen noodles.

Sort of.

Are you hungry?

Madagascar 馬達加斯加

The trunk is too thick to climb.

Hold tight!

No wonder the baobab tree is the largest tree in the country.

1 Hold tight! 堅持下去！

2 No wonder 難怪

New Zealand 紐西蘭

New Zealand is full of sheep!

It's getting warmer now. Let's shear the sheep.

They've set me free!

Baa baa

Wool

1 Shear the sheep 剃羊毛

2 Set me free 還我自由

Russia 俄羅斯

1. **Hide-and-seek** 捉迷藏

2. **Why not?** 好啊！

3. **Nesting dolls** 俄羅斯套娃

South Africa 南非

Welcome to the Kruger National Park! We have mighty animals here like me!

ROAR!

Oh, that's scary. Leg it!

1 Mighty 強大的

2 ROAR! 吼！（咆哮的聲音）

3 Leg it! 快跑！（用於意外的情況）

The ancient Maya cities
瑪雅古城

1 Fall down 倒塌

2 Sense of humour 幽默感

United States of America 美國

I'm flying over the Grand Canyon. **Woo hoo!** Oh, is that a bear?

Yes, there are bears around…

…but only one is real.

United Kingdom 英國

1 Would you like some more tea? 你要加些茶嗎？

2 So do I. 我也一樣。

ET is coming to town!
外星人進城啦！

> Hi, penguin.
> It's nice to meet you.
> I'm an alien
> from far far away.

> This is my spaceship.
> It can take us
> to space.

> Do you want to
> come along?

> YES!
> I'd love to.

1 Do you want to come along?
你想一起來嗎？

2 I'd love to. 我很樂意。

Space 太空

> It's time to travel in space. Let's take a trip to the Moon!

1 Take a trip 去旅行

2 Astronaut 太空人

3 Float free 無重漂浮

> I'm an astronaut now.
> I need some 'space' to float free.

Floating around...

Hello my friend! 朋友，你好！

Yo! I'm African. Let's shake hands.

1. Indigenous 土生土長的

2. Shake hands 握手

3. Over (to you). 收到請回話。

4. Eye-opener 使人大開眼界的事物

I'm from the outer space, over.

Hey! I'm a polar bear living in the North Pole.

Making foreign friends can be a great eye-opener.

Buying souvenirs 買手信

1 Certainly! 當然啦！ **2** Too tight 太緊了

Sending postcard 寄明信片

Mushroom
Unit A, 17/F,
78 Hung To Road,
Kwun Tong, Kowloon
Hong Kong

I'm going to send a postcard to my friend.
See, I put my penguin stamp on it.

Ding Ding,
you need a
postage stamp
instead.

1 Stamp 印章 / 郵票

2 Instead 作為替代

I want to see the world!
我想看看外面的世界！

There are so many places in the world for us to explore. Why not go on an adventure?

That's dangerous! Don't do that ever again.

OH! I'm trapped. I can't go anywhere.

1 Go on an adventure 去冒險

2 I'm trapped. 我被困了。 **3** Don't do that ever again. 別再這樣做了。

有情有境
學英語 **05** 世界篇 Hello W

原作	江記（江康泉）
撰文	閱亮點編輯室
內容總監	曾玉英
責任編輯	Zeny Lam
顧問編輯	Sarah E.Williams
書籍設計	Stephen Chan

出版　　　閱亮點有限公司 Enrich Spot Limited
　　　　　九龍觀塘鴻圖道 78 號 17 樓 A 室
發行　　　天窗出版社有限公司 Enrich Publishing Ltd.
　　　　　九龍觀塘鴻圖道 78 號 17 樓 A 室
電話　　　(852) 2793 5678
傳真　　　(852) 2793 5030
網址　　　www.enrichculture.com
電郵　　　info@enrichculture.com
出版日期　2021 年 12 月初版

承印　　　嘉昱有限公司
　　　　　九龍新蒲崗大有街 26-28 號天虹大廈 7 字樓

定價　　　港幣 $88　新台幣 $440
國際書號　978-988-75704-5-5
圖書分類　(1) 兒童圖書　　(2) 英語學習

DING DING

ding_ding_penguin